D0236381

BRISBANE

**IN MODERN
ENGLISH**

The Pilgrim's Progress

IN MODERN
ENGLISH

**Retold by Jean Watson
From the Story by John Bunyan**

Illustrated by Peter Wane

Galley Press

The Pilgrims Progress in Modern English
Copyright © 1978 by Scripture Union
Illustrations copyright © 1978 by Scripture Union

This edition published 1980 by special arrangement with
Scripture Union, London, England.

Reprinted 1981

ISBN 0 86136 086 9

All rights reserved. No part of this publication may be reproduced, stored in a retrieval system, or
transmitted, in any form or by any means, electronic, mechanical, photocopying, recording or otherwise, without the prior permission of the publisher, except for brief quotations in literary reviews.

Printed and bound in Great Britain by
William Clowes (Beccles) Limited, Beccles and London

CONTENTS

Who would true valour see
Let him come hither;
One here will constant be,
Come wind, come weather;
There's no discouragement
Shall make him once relent
His first avowed intent
To be a pilgrim.

Whoso beset him round
With dismal stories,
Do but themselves confound;
His strength the more is.
No foes shall stay his might,
Though he with giants fight;
He will make good his right
To be a pilgrim.

Hobgoblin nor foul fiend
Can daunt his spirit,
He knows he at the end
Shall life inherit.
Then fancies flee away!
I'll fear not what men say;
I'll labour night and day
To be a pilgrim.

1.
THE CITY OF DESTRUCTION

his is the story of a disturbing dream. It began in the City of Destruction. In that doomed place lived a man called Christian.

One day, deeply distressed, his shoulders bowed under the weight of a huge burden, Christian stood outside his house, reading a book, whose contents made him weep and tremble. From time to time he would cry out, 'What shall I do?' Eventually, he turned and entered his home. For a time he managed to behave normally in front of his wife and children but at last he broke down and told them of his despair. 'This burden is crippling me,' he began, 'and I'm also tormented by the knowledge that our city will be burnt and all of us with it – unless we find a way to escape.'

At these words, Christian's family stared incredulously at him. Then, concluding that the poor man was ill, they put him to bed. But Christian could not sleep and by morning was more miserable than ever. His relatives did everything possible to drive away his gloom. They tried scolding, teasing, ignoring him even, but none of their efforts succeeded.

Bowed by his burden, Christian spent his time alone, either weeping and praying in his room or pacing the countryside studying his book. At last one day, half-way across a wide field, he came to a halt, and cried out in despair, 'What must I do to be saved?'

As if in answer to his question, a white-robed man, Evangelist by name, approached Christian, and asked, 'Why do you weep?'
'Because this book warns me of death and future judgement and I am ready for neither,' Christian replied.

Then Evangelist drew out and unrolled a parchment which contained the words: 'Flee from the wrath to come.' Seeing this, Christian begged the old man to tell him where he should run. In reply, Evangelist pointed into the distance.

'Do you see that wicket gate?'

'No.'

'Well, then, do you see that shining light?'

'I think I do.'

'Keep looking at that light and go on walking towards it until you see the gate. Approach it and knock.'

At these words, a ray of hope penetrated Christian's despair and he began to run, in spite of his huge burden, towards the light.

'Come back! Come back to us!' his wife and children and their neighbours implored him, but Christian put his hands over his ears and quickened his pace, shouting, 'Life! Eternal Life!'

Obstinate and Pliable, two of Christian's neighbours, not content with shouting after him, decided to follow him and bring him back by force. They soon caught him up.

'Why have you come?' Christian demanded.

'To persuade you to return with us,' they replied.

'I can't do that!' Christian insisted. 'The City of Destruction is doomed; so are we – if we stay there. Why don't you come with me?'

'What – and leave all our friends and comforts behind?' asked Obstinate in astonishment.

'They are nothing, compared with all the joys ahead of us,' answered Christian eagerly.

'What joys?' demanded Obstinate.

'A heavenly home and city,' Christian explained. 'A place that's pure and perfect and will last for ever.' Pointing to his book he added, 'You can read about it, here.'

'Bother your book!' said Obstinate testily. 'Will you return with us or not?'

'I will not,' Christian answered decisively.

'Come, Pliable,' said Obstinate, turning away from Christian. 'Let's leave this conceited, stubborn fellow and return home.'

But Pliable answered, 'What if Christian's hopes are true? I feel inclined to go along with him!'

Then Obstinate urged his neighbour to go back to the City of Destruction with him, and Christian invited him to go on to Mount Zion.

Pliable hesitated, then came to a decision. 'I'll take my chance with Christian,' he said.

'In that case, I'll go home,' declared Obstinate. 'I refuse to stay with a couple of deluded fools!'

As this stubborn gentleman turned and headed for the City of Destruction, Christian and Pliable walked, side-by-side, in the direction of the light. Happy at having found a companion, Christian talked eagerly to Pliable about the joys ahead of them. 'In the eternal city, to which we are travelling, live God and his angels, as well as martyrs and other pilgrims,' he said.

The travellers were so engrossed in conversation that they did not notice, until it was too late, the boggy ground that lay across their path. Soon both men were wallowing waist-high in the mud and filth of a swamp, called the Slough of Despond. Pliable, by nature easily discouraged, struggled to reach the nearside bank, reproaching Christian with the words, 'Is this the joy you promised me? I dread to think what dangers lie ahead! If I get out of this bog alive, you can go on, alone, to your precious city!' Regaining the safety of the bank,

Pliable headed for the City of Destruction, leaving his companion to flounder in the swamp, whose boggy condition was maintained by the fears and doubts of those who became conscious of their sins. Here Christian might have remained, but for the aid of a man called Help, who took his hand and pulled him clear. Grateful to be on the right road again, the muddy pilgrim trudged on towards the light.

Before long, he met another traveller – Worldly Wiseman, from the Town of Worldly Wisdom, near the City of Destruction.

'Where are you going, weary traveller?' Worldly Wiseman greeted Christian.

'To the gate – to be freed from my burden,' was the reply.

'Who told you to go this way?'

'Evangelist.'

'I might have known!' snorted Worldly Wiseman. 'This is a

dangerous route. You have already encountered the Slough of Despond; if you continue on this road, you will face weariness and pain, dragons and darkness, death and many other dangers.'

'But my burden is worse than any of the things you've mentioned,' insisted Christian.

'And how did you acquire your burden in the first place?'

'By reading this book.'

'Meddling in matters beyond one's understanding always leads to confusion and despair,' admonished Worldly Wiseman, 'but I can show you an easier way to find release. In the nearby village of Morality, lives a man called Legality and his charming son, Civility. They are such good people! Legality will soon remove your load, and then you can send for your family and settle down to live a decent, moral life among honest neighbours.'

Christian hesitated, then said, 'Show me the way to this good man's house.'

Worldly Wiseman gave clear directions.

'See that high hill?' he asked, pointing away from the path. 'Go past it and you will see Morality Village. The first house belongs to Legality.'

Hopefully at first, Christian approached the hill, but as he came closer to it, he feared that the overhanging ridge would fall on him. This fear, and the apparently increased weight of his burden, made the pilgrim stand still. In this state of perplexity, he looked up and saw flames erupting from the hillside. At this Christian broke out in a cold sweat, and shook with fear, regretting that he had followed bad advice and ashamed that Evangelist, whom he now saw rapidly approaching, should find him there.

Coming up to Christian, Evangelist asked sternly, 'What are you doing here?'

The pilgrim admitted that he had listened to the words of Worldly Wiseman.

'Now listen to God's words,' Evangelist commanded. 'He says he cannot delight in one who turns aside from the way of truth.'

Overcome by shame and fear, Christian sank to the ground, but his guide quickly lifted him up and reassured him, 'God will forgive all sin, so you must not doubt – but believe!'

Then Christian listened humbly as Evangelist explained why Worldly Wiseman was an enemy, Legality a cheat and Civility a hypocrite.

'Worldly Wiseman is only wise in the ways of this world. He wants to turn men away from the road that leads to the cross, directing them to the path that leads to death. You must reject all his false advice. As for Legality, he cannot remove your load. He has never freed anyone from the burden of his sin; indeed, he cannot, since no one ever succeeds in fulfilling all the law's demands throughout his life.'

Having spoken, Evangelist called on heaven to verify his words. Immediately, flames spurted from the hill and a voice thundered, 'Those who depend on the law are under a curse.'

KNOCK AND IT SHALL BE OPENED UNTO YOU

Overcome with remorse, Christian asked, fearfully, 'Is there any hope for me? Will my sin be forgiven?'

'You have failed,' agreed Evangelist, 'but the man at the gate will welcome you, for he wishes everyone well. Only, don't turn aside again from the right way.'

The wise guide then embraced the pilgrim and, smiling, wished him 'Godspeed.'

With renewed courage and determination, Christian strode forward, glancing neither right nor left. On reaching the wicket gate he stopped and read the words written above it: 'Knock and it shall be opened unto you.'

Trembling with excitement, dirt and tiredness forgotten, the traveller raised a hand and knocked.

2.
INTERPRETER'S HOUSE

othing happened until Christian had knocked and called out several times. Then a voice asked, 'Who are you? Where are you from? What do you want?' The pilgrim replied, 'I am a burdened sinner on my way to Mount Zion from the City of Destruction, and I want to know whether you will let me in.'

'Come in!' With these welcoming words, the gate was opened and,

to Christian's surprise, a hand jerked him over the threshold. Face to face with Goodwill, the gatekeeper, he demanded, 'Why did you pull me in like that?'

'To save you from Beelzebub's sharp arrows,' answered Goodwill. 'His grim castle stands close by, and his soldiers aim their arrows at pilgrims who approach the gate – hoping to kill them before they are admitted.' Then the gatekeeper questioned Christian about the people and dangers he had encountered.

When the pilgrim had given an account of his adventures, Goodwill pointed ahead saying, 'Do you see that narrow way? It's the path you must now take; a route pioneered by the prophets, Christ and his apostles; a straight and narrow way.'

Christian studied the path ahead. 'Are there no turnings or bends?' he asked.

'There are many by-ways,' Goodwill replied, 'but all of them are wide and crooked, so you will know they are not to be followed.'

Ever conscious of the weight on his back, Christian asked, 'Can you not help me to be rid of my burden?'

'You must bear it a little longer,' Goodwill told him.

Then he directed the pilgrim to Interpreter's house, adding the instruction, 'Go up to the door and knock.'

After knocking several times, Christian was admitted and welcomed by Interpreter. Following a man with a lighted candle, the pilgrim and his host went into a room. As the light-bearer opened a door, Christian's eyes were immediately attracted to a picture hanging on a wall behind it. This depicted a figure with a book in his hands, a crown above his head and the world behind his back. The figure was that of a man – but such a man as Christian had never seen before.

He was perfection in human shape: love emanated from his eyes; truth was imprinted on his lips; eternal wisdom and innocence radiated from his face.

'What does this picture mean?' asked Christian, awed.

'The person it depicts is unique,' Interpreter replied. 'He offers light and truth to sinners. He forsook the world for the love of God and for the joys ahead. He is the only one who can guide you through the difficult places on your route.'

Deeply moved, Christian followed his guide into a dusty room. At

Interpreter's command, a man began to sweep the floor vigorously, but the only result of his efforts was to envelop himself and the bystanders in clouds of dust.

'Do you understand?' Interpreter asked, and then explained, 'This room is like the sinner's life, the dust – his sin, and the man who sweeps the floor – the law. The sweeper stirs up the dust but cannot sweep it away. Similarly, the law makes a sinner more aware of his wrong-doings but it cannot help him to be free of them.'

Next Interpreter asked a girl standing nearby to bring some water. She obeyed and then sprinkled the water all over the room. When the dust had settled, it was easy for the floor to be swept quite clean. 'The good news of the Saviour is like that water,' Interpreter said. 'Those who receive it are made clean and ready for the presence of the King.'

Christian was then taken into another room to watch two children. One, named Patience, was calm and contented; the other, Passion, could not conceal his restlessness and impatience. A bag was brought in and its contents – a hoard of glittering treasures – emptied near Passion, who seized the bright jewels in frenzied pleasure, laughing at empty-handed Patience.

But the scene soon changed, revealing a much altered Passion. He had squandered all his treasures, and he now stood clothed in nothing but rags and sunk in gloom. Patience, however, still sat in an attitude of calm hope.

'Passion is like the person who wants to have his fill of pleasure while he lives on earth,' said Interpreter. 'Patience is like the traveller to Zion, who turns his back on worldly pleasures and waits with patience for the unfading joys of heaven.'

Determined to remember the example of Patience, Christian then
followed Interpreter to a wall, against which a fire blazed higher and
hotter every moment, although a man stood nearby, throwing water
over the flames. As he watched, the pilgrim understood why; hidden
by the wall another man was feeding the flames with oil. 'The fire is
like God's work in people's lives,' Interpreter expounded. 'The devil,
represented by the man with water, wants to quench it, but he cannot,
for Christ, the other man, keeps feeding the flame of new life with the
oil of his love and kindness.'

Christian tried to fix the details of this encouraging scene in his mind.

Then Interpreter showed Christian a castle. The pilgrim was delighted by its grandeur and beauty. He longed to be among the gold-clad figures walking along its battlements.

But the door into the castle was guarded by armed men whose presence discouraged those who wanted to enter from doing so. In the courtyard, a scribe sat at a table, writing down in a book the names of the people who filed slowly past him. As Christian surveyed this

scene, he noticed a man whose uncowed bearing marked him out from the rest. Walking boldly up to the table, this man said firmly, 'Write down my name, sir!' As soon as the scribe had done so, the man put on his helmet, drew his sword and rushed at the armed guard, laying about him with such strength and determination that, in spite of receiving many wounds, he managed to cut his way right into the castle.

'Come in! Come in! Eternal glory you will win,' sang the gold-clad figures on the battlements as the victor entered and was given his own gold robe.

This happy sight made Christian long to be on his way again, but Interpreter said, 'I have more to show you. Come!'

He led the pilgrim to a dark room in which stood an iron cage. Christian noticed, with horror, its pitiful occupant: a man, sitting in an attitude of despair, eyes downcast and hands folded, occasionally letting out heart-breaking sighs. 'Who are you?' Christian asked him. The man, whose name was Backslider, answered, 'I am not the person I once was.'

'Who was that?'

'A wise and happy believer, bound for the Celestial City,' was the reply.

'And what are you now?'

'A man imprisoned by despair, shut up for ever in this cage.'

'How did you get into the cage?'

'I failed to keep guard against the evil one, and took my pleasures where and when I wished,' the wretched prisoner answered. 'I sinned against God and his Spirit. Now God has left me and the devil has come in his place.'

Christian was filled with pity for the speaker.

'The Son of the King is merciful,' he pointed out, but nothing could penetrate Backslider's despair.

'I am shut up in this cage with the terror of coming judgement as my companion,' he intoned.

'Let this man's misery be a warning to you,' said Interpreter as he and Christian walked away.

'God keep me always on my guard,' the pilgrim prayed.

By now Christian was longing to be on his way but his guide had one more object-lesson for him. Taking him into another room, he showed Christian a man rising from bed and beginning to dress.

By name Unready, this man was in a state of terror.

'Why does he tremble so?' Christian asked.

Prompted by Interpreter, Unready answered the pilgrim's question. 'Last night I had a dream in which I saw the sky grow dark with fast-scudding clouds. Thunder boomed and jagged lightning streaked across the blackness. In my fear, I looked upwards and saw, framed in fire, thousands of angels, all attending a Man who sat upon a cloud. After a trumpet's blare, a voice boomed, "Arise you dead, and come to judgement."

'At once, rocks split and graves opened, releasing the dead; some advanced with joy shining from their upturned faces, but the rest slunk off to hide themselves in rocks and holes. Then, opening a book, the Man proceeded to judge the world. Again a voice rang out, addressing the angel-attendants: "Burn the chaff!" Immediately, at my feet, there gaped a bottomless pit from which burning coals, smoke and hideous sounds erupted. The next command resounded: "Gather the wheat into the barn!" At these words, many people were caught up and carried into the clouds. I was not among them. Left

behind, I tried to hide, but everywhere I went the eyes of that Man followed me. Then I woke up.'

'Why were you so afraid of this dream?' Christian enquired.

Unready answered, with a shudder, 'Because I thought the Day of Judgement had really come and I had been unprepared for it. As Hell gaped at my feet, and that Man's eyes looked at me, I remembered my sins, and their guilt was more than I could bear.'

After this sight, Interpreter asked Christian whether he had considered all he had seen and heard.

'Yes, each lesson has been either an encouragement or a warning to me,' the pilgrim replied.

'Let the memory of all you have experienced here spur you on,' his guide exhorted him.

Leaving Interpreter's house, Christian, thoughtful but eager, continued along the straight and narrow way.

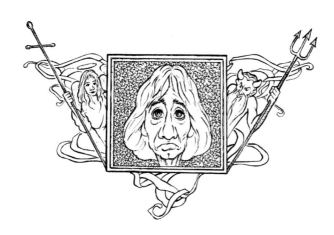

3.
LIFE

oon his path lay between two thick, protective walls named Salvation. Though the going was rough, Christian began to run up the steep track, for he could see, a little way ahead, a cross, and underneath that a grave. To reach the cross was the pilgrim's burning aim. And the moment he breasted the rise on which the wooden stake and crosspiece stood his burden dropped off his back and thudded to the ground. He watched it roll and tumble down the slope until it fell into the open grave and disappeared from sight. With that load went all the fear and guilt which Christian had been carrying for so long. Tears of relief and joy coursed down his cheeks. He gazed at the cross upon which he thought he saw a man hanging, and murmured, 'He has given me rest by his sorrow and life by his death.'

Three Shining Ones appeared, saying, 'Peace be to you.' The first one added, 'Your sins are forgiven.' The second one stripped him of his rags and gave him a new robe and coat. The third one put a mark on his forehead and a scroll in his hands with the instruction, 'Read this as you run and present it when you reach the Celestial City.'

The Shining Ones vanished but Christian's joy remained, making him leap three times in the air before going on his way, singing.

Happy in his new-found liberty and peace, Christian descended to a valley, where he soon came across three men with chains on their heels lying asleep by the path. Alarmed at their vulnerable position, he stopped to rouse them. 'It's not safe to sleep here,' he said, shaking them. 'At any moment the devil might pass by, like a roaring lion, and seize you as his prey. Wake up and let me help you to remove your chains!'

Simple yawned, sat up and looked round, sleepily.

'I see no danger,' he mumbled.

Sloth opened his eyes and murmured, 'A little more sleep.'

Presumption woke up long enough to tell Christian to let each man mind his own business. Then he and the other two men went back to sleep. Puzzled and saddened that his advice and help had been rejected without a moment's serious thought, Christian continued through the valley.

Before long, his attention was attracted by two men, Formalist and Hypocrisy, who came scrambling over a wall just ahead.

'Where have you come from and where are you going?' Christian greeted them.

'From the Land of Vainglory to Mount Zion,' they replied.

'But why didn't you come through the gate at the beginning of the way?' asked Christian.

Formalist and Hypocrisy pointed out that climbing over the wall was much quicker.

'But, in taking this short-cut, aren't you disobeying the Lord of the City towards which we are travelling?'

'Don't worry about that!' was the confident reply. 'For more than a thousand years people have been using this short-cut, and a custom which has been observed for so long must surely rate as law. Does it matter *how* we got here? Now that we're on the way, what's the difference between you and us?'

'I'm walking in obedience to God's laws; you're following your own ideas,' answered Christian.

This made Formalist and Hypocrisy look at each other and laugh. After that, they kept to themselves and did not speak to Christian again. Left on his own once more, the pilgrim kept taking out and reading his scroll.

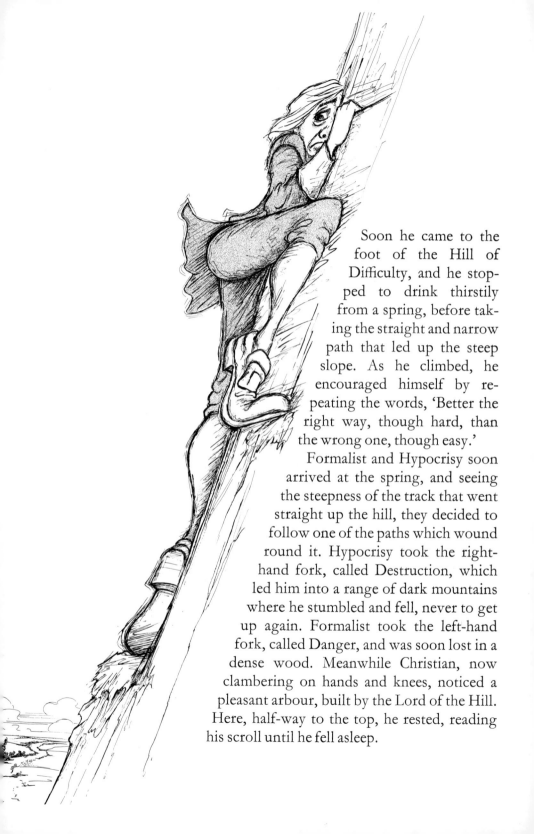

Soon he came to the foot of the Hill of Difficulty, and he stopped to drink thirstily from a spring, before taking the straight and narrow path that led up the steep slope. As he climbed, he encouraged himself by repeating the words, 'Better the right way, though hard, than the wrong one, though easy.'

Formalist and Hypocrisy soon arrived at the spring, and seeing the steepness of the track that went straight up the hill, they decided to follow one of the paths which wound round it. Hypocrisy took the right-hand fork, called Destruction, which led him into a range of dark mountains where he stumbled and fell, never to get up again. Formalist took the left-hand fork, called Danger, and was soon lost in a dense wood. Meanwhile Christian, now clambering on hands and knees, noticed a pleasant arbour, built by the Lord of the Hill. Here, half-way to the top, he rested, reading his scroll until he fell asleep.

He slept till nearly nightfall, when he was roused by a voice which chided him for his sloth. With a guilty start, Christian jumped up and continued on his way. On the road ahead he saw two men, Mistrust and Timorous, hurrying down the hill.

Christian called out to them, 'You're going the wrong way. What's the matter?'

'We *were* on our way to Mount Zion,' replied Timorous, shakily, 'but the further we go, the greater the difficulties we encounter, so we have decided to turn back.'

Mistrust took up the story. 'In our path lie a couple of lions who will surely tear us apart.'

Infected by their fear, Christian stood still, wondering what to do, but a moment's thought showed him that it was better to go forward, fearing death but knowing that life in the Celestial City lay beyond it, than to go back to certain doom. Accordingly, he continued up the hill as Timorous and Mistrust sped down it. Soon afterwards, feeling the need for comfort, the pilgrim put a hand inside his coat but found, to his horror, that the scroll was not in its usual place. 'Where could it be?' he wondered, frantically. Then he remembered reading it in the arbour before he had fallen asleep. Begging God to forgive him for his carelessness, Christian retraced his steps to the arbour, looking

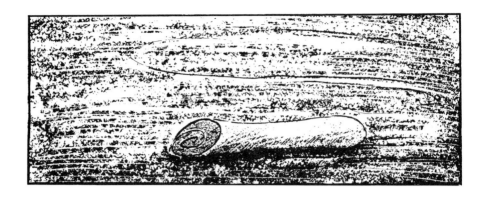

anxiously but fruitlessly at the ground all the way. Then, sitting on the bench in the arbour, he wept.

After he'd stopped crying, he noticed, lying under the seat, but still intact, the precious parchment, which must have slipped out of his hands as he'd slept. Joyfully, the pilgrim retrieved it and put it back in his coat, remembering to thank God for helping him to recover this source of comfort and assurance. Then, for the second time, he climbed the upper slopes of the hill, but by now the sun had set, and the traveller deeply regretted all the daylight hours he had wasted in sleep. His fears of lions and other lurking dangers grew with the dark. When a large building became visible just ahead, he decided, if he could, to obtain a night's lodging there. Seeing the porter's lodge at the end of a narrow alley-way, he began to approach it, until daunting sights and sounds brought him to a sudden halt. Two ferocious-looking lions, one on each side of the alley, crouched, growling and snarling at him. Terrified, Christian realised these must be the beasts which had made Mistrust and Timorous turn tail and run. The pilgrim might well have followed their example, had not Watchful, the porter, called out at that moment, 'Do not fear the lions, for they are chained. Keep walking in the middle of the path and you will not be harmed!' As he obeyed, Christian discovered that the chained beasts could do nothing but roar, so, clapping his hands boldly, he went past them and up to the porter's lodge, where he was admitted by kindly Watchful. Christian then explained why he had arrived so late, and requested a night's lodging. At this, Watchful pulled a bell-rope, saying, 'I'll call one of the caretakers.'

Answering the summons, a graceful girl called Discretion entered the room and began talking to Christian. She called her sisters, Piety, Prudence and Charity, to come and join her. Quickly convinced of Christian's credentials, these wise and gentle keepers of the mansion led him from the lodge to the main house saying, 'Come in, for this house was built by the Lord of the Hill in order to help pilgrims like yourself.' So Christian entered the huge and lovely building known as the Palace Beautiful. When the five of them had made themselves comfortable, the caretakers asked the traveller for more details about himself, his family and his journey, and Christian answered all their questions fully and truthfully.

At the pleasant evening meal which followed, the sisters told their guest more about the Lord of the Hill.

'He is a brave warrior, who, at great cost to himself, fought and killed the one who had the power of death. Some of our household have seen him since his death and can assure you that he loves pilgrims very dearly. He stripped himself of his glory in order to give eternal riches to the poor and humble, and to make heavenly princes out of earthly pilgrims.'

That night Christian slept in a bedroom named Peace, and in the morning woke up feeling so happy that he broke into song. For a few days he stayed to explore the palace. One room contained relics and mementoes of the journeyings of the Lord of the Hill and many pilgrims. Among these objects, he saw David's sling and Gideon's pitcher.

In another room, Christian marvelled at the array of swords, shields, breast-plates, helmets and other kinds of armour provided for pilgrims by the Lord of the Hill. One morning, his companions took him to the palace roof and pointed out, in the distance, the Delectable Mountains and the woods and waters of Immanuel's Land.

The following day, after fitting him from head to foot with armour, the sisters accompanied their guest to the bottom of the hill, where they gave him food and good advice before bidding him farewell. Christian set off at once, eager to catch up with Faithful, a fellow-countryman whom Watchful had seen passing the Palace Beautiful some time earlier. But first, the pilgrim had to face a new and deadly danger.

4.
THE SHADOW
OF DEATH

elow the hill lay the Valley of Humiliation. On his way through this depressing hollow, Christian saw a fearful demon bearing down on him. It was Apollyon. Terrified but determined, Christian stood his ground as the towering monster roared at him, 'Where are you from?'

'The City of Destruction,' was the pilgrim's reply.

'Then you're mine, for that place belongs to me!' snarled the fiend. 'Why are you running away from me, your king?'

'I found your service hard and your wages worse,' answered Christian, 'for the wages of sin are death.'

'Go back to your country,' urged Apollyon, 'and I will see what can be done about your pay and conditions of service.'

'But I have pledged my service to the Prince of princes,' the pilgrim pointed out.

'Then you have changed a bad situation for a worse one,' stated his enemy. 'But it's not too late. Many who profess to serve this Prince return to my service after a time. You'd be well advised to do the same.'

'No!' answered Christian. 'For I far prefer his service and rewards, his servants and government, his company and country, to yours. Stop trying to persuade me to turn back, for I will follow my Prince.'

Barely able to conceal his annoyance, Apollyon urged the pilgrim to reconsider. 'Just think of all his servants who come to bad ends! Your Prince does nothing to avert these situations!' he said.

'If he does not rescue them, it is to test their love,' Christian countered. 'Nor is it true that his servants' lives end in tragedy, for all of them will share the Prince's glory, when he and his angels return.'

Apollyon's next tactic was to catalogue the pilgrim's failures. 'You almost choked in the Slough of Despond and would have tried wrong ways of being free of your burden,' he accused Christian. 'You slept on the way and lost your precious scroll. You were terrified by lions and are entirely motivated by a desire for your own glory!'

'Everything you say is true and there is more besides,' admitted Christian, 'but I have repented of these sins, and obtained forgiveness for all my wrong-doings from the merciful Prince whom I serve.'

No longer able to hide his true nature and purpose, Apollyon raged, 'I hate the Prince, his laws and people and I have come to fight you!'

'Beware!' Christian warned him. 'I am on the King's highway, the way of holiness.' But Apollyon swelled to his full size and straddled the path hurling a flaming dart at Christian, who fended it off with his shield, as he hastily drew his two-edged sword. For half a day they fought. It was a grisly battle. The foul fiend, yelling and roaring, peppered his opponent with fiery darts, and Christian, groaning and panting, defended himself with his shield as he cut and thrust with his attacking sword. At one point, weakened by wounds in his head, hands and feet, the pilgrim staggered backwards. Immediately, the scaly beast seized the chance to come to grips with his opponent. A fearful wrestling match ensued, and at last Apollyon managed to bring Christian crashing to the ground with such force that the two-edged sword flew out of his hand. Then, sensing victory, Apollyon closed in for the kill, but, just as the fiend raised his hand to deliver a final, fatal blow, Christian regained his sword and thrust it forcefully upwards, shouting, 'Rejoice not against me, O mine enemy; when I fall, I shall arise!' Taken by surprise, the evil beast stumbled backwards, and his adversary followed up his advantage by attacking with renewed vigour, shouting in triumph, 'In all these things we have complete victory through him who loved us.' When the final outcome was inevitable, the defeated arch-enemy of God spread his wings and flew away.

Then the weak but happy victor sang a song of thanks to God for his help in the battle. At the end of the song, a hand appeared, holding leaves from the tree of life. Christian took and applied these to his wounds, and found immediate relief and healing. After that he ate and

drank from the provisions given to him by the caretakers of the Palace Beautiful. Feeling fit and well again, the pilgrim got up and continued with his journey. As a wise precaution, he held a drawn sword in his hand, although, in fact, he reached the valley's end without further trouble.

Directly in Christian's path, lay another valley: the Valley of the Shadow of Death. As Christian neared this, two men came running out of the entrance, shouting, 'Back! Back!'

'What's the matter?' asked the pilgrim, alarmed.

'That valley!' they gasped. 'If we'd gone any further down it we wouldn't have lived to tell the tale! You have never seen the like of the hobgoblins, satyrs and dragons that haunt it, or heard anything to equal the harrowing hisses, yells and howls that fill the air. Discouragement and confusion hang there in clouds and death spreads its wings over the hellish hollow.'

'Yet I must go this way – it's on my route,' said Christian. Then, turning his back on the fleeing figures of the two men, the pilgrim stepped forward. On reaching the valley's mouth he quickly

ascertained that the reports he had received about the terrors of the valley had not been exaggerated. In addition, the narrow path along which he must travel was flanked by a deep ditch to the left and a wide quagmire to the right.

Fearfully, hesitantly, the pilgrim groped forward into deepening darkness. Each step brought him nearer to a place more chilling than anything he had yet encountered.

In the middle of the valley there yawned the mouth of Hell itself. Approaching this, Christian heard blood-curdling shrieks and saw flames and smoke. He knew that he must now sheathe his sword and put on the armour of All-Prayer. Having done this, the pilgrim cried out, 'I beg you, Lord, save me,' and edged slowly past fingers of flame which clawed at him as if they would tear away his flesh, while agonised cries rang in his ears. In addition to these horrors, Christian was aware of forces, like mighty winds, which rushed to and fro, and which, he feared, might tear him limb from limb or trample over him. For several miles he managed to keep moving forward in spite of these grim sights, sounds and sensations, but when he heard a pack of fiends approaching, his courage failed and he stopped, frozen with fear. In this emergency reason came to his rescue, reminding him that it would be as dangerous to retreat as to advance, and so the pilgrim pressed on shouting, 'I will walk in the strength of the Lord God.' At this the fiends fell back, allowing Christian to pass by, though not unscathed, for one evil and malicious spirit crept up behind and whispered blasphemies in the traveller's ear. In his confusion, Christian assumed that the profane thoughts were the product of his own imagination, and so self-loathing was added to his other torments. In this tortured frame of mind, he continued along the way for some time, but his spirits rose a little when he heard a voice quoting, 'Though I walk through the valley of the shadow of death, I will fear no evil, for thou art with me.' It seemed to be coming from somewhere just ahead of him.

Encouraged by this reminder of God's presence and by the thought that he was just behind another traveller to Zion, Christian quickened his step and soon found himself emerging into light. As full morning broke, the pilgrim sang out, joyfully, 'He has turned the shadow of death into morning.' Then he turned around and saw, by the light of

day, the unmitigated horrors of the ditch and quagmire, the hob-goblins and satyrs which lay behind him. But there were fresh dangers ahead, as he quickly realised when he turned to survey the second half of the valley, which was, if possible, more hazardous than the first. If he had had to negotiate its snares and traps, pits and holes in the darkness, he would certainly have blundered. Instead, in the full light of day, he advanced boldly, avoiding every obstacle, and the words that filled his thoughts were these: 'God was always with me then and gave me light as I walked through darkness.'

Almost at the valley's end, Christian was confronted by another grisly sight. On the ground were blood-stains, heaps of ashes, scattered bones and the mangled bodies of former pilgrims. Nearby, in the mouth of a cave, sat two forbidding-looking giants, Pope and Pagan by name. However, Christian by-passed their gruesome den without difficulty, for Pagan had been dead for several years and Pope was old and powerless.

With the long, dark valley behind him, the pilgrim proceeded cheerfully, singing of his deliverance.

5.
FAITHFUL

reasting a rise, Christian saw Faithful ahead and shouted, 'Wait!' At this, the latter looked back but dared not stop walking, so Christian had to run until he managed to overtake his fellow-countryman. Pleased with himself, Christian took his eyes off the path and promptly stumbled and fell. Faithful hurried to his side and

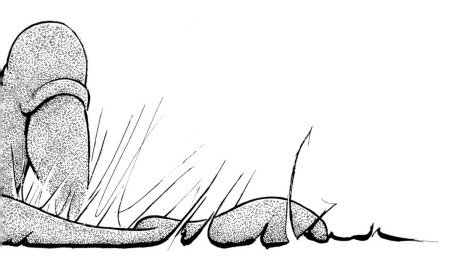

helped him up. The pilgrims' joy at finding each other quickly outweighed the effects of this small accident, and they travelled on in high spirits. Having left the City of Destruction more recently than Christian, Faithful was able to give news of Pliable's reception by the city's inhabitants; ever since his return these folk had mocked and abused him for backing out of his journey. But this topic was far less engrossing than a comparison of their own adventures, so Christian and Faithful proceeded to recount their experiences to one another as they journeyed along.

Christian was interested to learn that although Faithful had avoided the Slough of Despond, he had faced a different temptation in the comely shape of Wanton, who tried to entice him with carnal pleasures. Only by closing his eyes against her bewitching looks, had the pilgrim managed to pass her by unscathed.

At the foot of the Hill of Difficulty, he had met Adam-the-First, from the Town of Deceit. This old man had offered Faithful a job, assuring him that he would find the work delightful and that his wages would be to inherit, in due course, all that Adam owned.

In answer to some questions from the pilgrim, the old man had added that his house was furnished with every possible luxury, and that Faithful would be free to marry, should he so wish, all Adam's three daughters: the Lust-of-the-Flesh, the Lust-of-the-Eyes and the Pride-of-Life.

'To begin with I was tempted by Adam-the-First's offer,' admitted Faithful, 'but then I noticed the words on his forehead: "Reject the old man with his deeds." In a flash of insight, I realised Adam's real intention was to sell me as a slave, so I turned him down. At this he became abusive, threatening to send someone after me to beat me up. When I turned to leave him the old man pinched me so hard that I thought he had torn away some of my flesh.'

After this encounter, Faithful, conscious all the time of being followed, had climbed the Hill of Difficulty. At the arbour, he had come face-to-face with his pursuer, whom he had recognised as Moses. Without a word, this severe law-giver had knocked Faithful down, and proceeded to beat and punch him with such vigour that death might have resulted, had not another man come by and forced the aggressor to stop and go away. Seeing the holes in the stranger's hands and side, Faithful had realised that his rescuer was the Lord. Then, full of gratitude, he had climbed up the hill and down the other side.

Down in the Valley of Humility, Faithful had encountered Discontent who had tried to persuade the pilgrim to turn back. 'He warned me,' Faithful told Christian, 'that there was no status or acclaim to be found in that valley, adding that if I did not go back, I'd offend my friends – Pride, Arrogance, Self-Conceit and Worldly-Glory. But I said these friends had disowned me when I'd become a pilgrim, and pointed out that humility must come before status.'

Christian discovered that Faithful had been accosted next by a gentleman named Shame, who had put forward the view that religion and humility were unmanly and shaming. 'At first I blushed, for his words made me feel foolish,'

Faithful confided, 'but when I remembered that men's foolishness is God's wisdom, I no longer felt ashamed of my Lord, my fellow-pilgrims or myself. But Shame stayed close to me, trying to make me change my mind, for a long time.'

Having finished recounting their adventures, the pilgrims turned their attention to a tall, good-looking man who had been walking on the other side of the road for some time. Faithful approached, and courteously invited this stranger to join them as they walked and talked. Almost at once, the man launched into a speech extolling the virtues of profitable conversation. 'Through wise words, a person can learn about the need for Christ and the new birth; about repentance and faith; about prayer and suffering,' he prattled. 'By means of words, one can also refute falsehood, vindicate truth and instruct the ignorant.'

Impressed by this high sounding flow of speech, Faithful returned to Christian's side and quietly voiced his good opinion of their prospective travelling companion. Smiling gently, Christian replied that the person he commended was a practised deceiver.

Then he explained to the surprised Faithful that he knew the man. 'His name is Talkative, the son of Say-Well, and he lives in Prating-Row in our City of Destruction,' he told his younger companion. 'When away from home, he's all sweetness and light, but while there, he's an ogre. Superficially he's pleasant, but on closer acquaintance he's most unattractive. His religion is all talk and no action; as an egg-white lacks flavour, so his religion lacks substance.'

Faithful, by now regretting his earlier impetuosity, asked Christian how they could shake off this unpleasant character, and was advised to ask Talkative some leading questions. Accordingly, Faithful approached the tall man and enquired, 'What are the evidences of God's work in a person's life?'

'First of all, the person will speak out strongly against sin,' began Talkative readily. He was about to make another point, when Faithful interrupted.

'Decrying sin is not enough; one must hate and shun it, too. But do go on.'

'Secondly,' resumed Talkative, 'the person will be knowledgeable about the truths of the gospel.'

Again Faithful pointed out the incompleteness of this answer. 'Knowing these truths is not enough; putting them into practice is essential, too,' he said. After this, the tall man fell grumpily silent, and was obliged to listen while his companion answered his own question about the effects of God's work in a person's life.

'The man himself will be deeply ashamed of his sin; this will make him come to the Saviour in repentance and faith, and thus experience a change of life and purpose. Others will hear his words and see a life-style that confirms them,' said Faithful, following up this speech by challenging Talkative with the questions, 'Have you experienced these things? Does your life measure up to your experience?'

The man replied testily that he declined to discuss topics like experience, conscience and God, and then withdrew from Christian and Faithful's company. These two pilgrims, however, continued to find satisfaction in each other's conversation, and to make good progress, even through a desert which lay on their route. At the end of this barren waste, the pilgrims looked back and spotted an old friend not far behind.

6.
VANITY FAIR

t was Evangelist. The pilgrims welcomed him, and he responded, 'I am very glad to find you still pursuing the right road, but I must warn you of the dangers ahead. In the next town, called Folly, you will be surrounded by enemies, and one of you will die. Beware, particularly, of the town's great attraction, Vanity Fair,

which Prince Beelzebub and his companions set up many years ago, with the intention of enticing pilgrims from the right way. In that fair, wealth and fame, pleasure and position, and many other follies, are for sale. Once, long ago, the Prince of princes passed through Folly, but he spent no time or money on its shoddy wares.'

Having said goodbye to Evangelist, Christian and Faithful proceeded into Folly Town, and so into Vanity Fair. Here, the pilgrims' strange dress and speech soon began to attract laughter and comment from the townsfolk. Christian and Faithful kept walking as long as they could, but when a jeering mob surrounded them, they were forced to stop. They bore, in silence, the crowd's mockery and insults, and offered no resistance when they were seized, and dragged along the streets into court, to be questioned by the magistrates. Here they were asked where they were going, where they came from and why they were dressed so strangely; to which Christian and Faithful responded courteously, 'We are pilgrims, on our way to the heavenly city, and have done nothing to cause this trouble.'

But the magistrates had already made up their minds that the pilgrims were mad, so they proceeded to beat them and smear them with dirt, then they pushed them into a cage to become the butt of staring eyes, pointing fingers and taunting voices. Christian and Faithful bore all this patiently, answering their tormentors gently and courteously. Some of the onlookers were softened by their behaviour, and tried to restrain their fellow townsfolk, but only succeeded in angering them more.

Tempers flared, and a scuffle broke out between the moderate and the violent groups. As a result, Christian and Faithful were taken to the magistrates for a second trial, at which they were made scapegoats for the disturbance. Their punishment was prolonged and severe. First they were beaten, then clamped in irons and chained, and finally led up and down the streets as a deterrent to others. But, through it all, Christian and Faithful showed such meekness and patience that, as before, some bystanders were won over. However, this so angered the rest that they resolved to bring about the pilgrims' deaths. In the meantime, they returned Christian and Faithful to the cage, making their feet fast in the stocks. Inside their humiliating prison, the

bruised and battered pilgrims comforted each other – remembering Evangelist's words – and then committed their future to God.

Later, the prisoners were released from the cage to be taken to their third trial. The presiding judge was Lord Hate-Good and he was assisted by twelve jurymen, whose names were these: Blind-Man, No-Good, Malice, Love-Lust, Live-Loose, Heady, High-Mind, Enmity, Liar, Cruelty, Hate-Light and Implacable.

Christian and Faithful stood before the judge and were charged with being enemies and peace-breakers.

It was Faithful who spoke up in defence of his companion and himself: 'We only reject whatever is in opposition to the Prince of princes,' he said, adding, 'my quarrel is with the Prince of Darkness. I defy him and all his angels.'

Next the three witnesses were called upon to state their accusations. First Envy stepped forward, and swore to tell the truth. He denounced Faithful with the words, 'That vile man says our views are opposed to Christianity.'

Next Superstition took the oath, and added his denunciation of Christian's companion. 'He says our religion is worthless because we cannot please God by it – and that must imply that we are all condemned.'

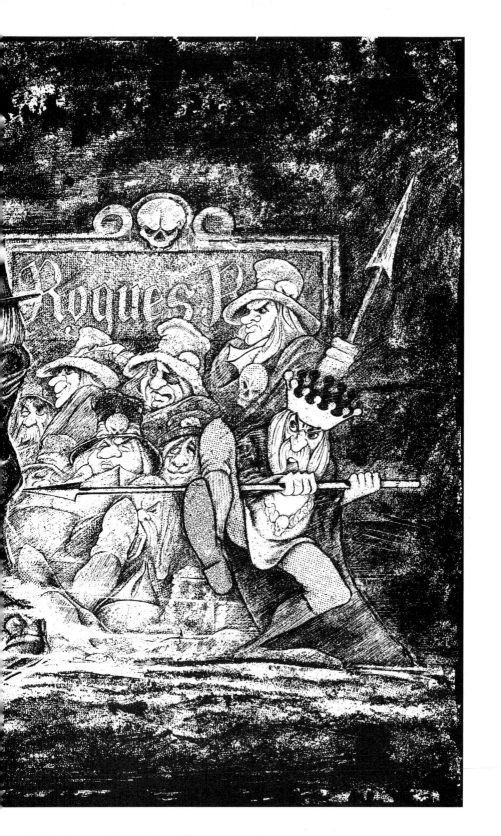

Finally, mealy-mouthed Pickthank was sworn in. 'The prisoner,' he said, indicating Faithful, 'speaks scornfully of our prince and also of you, my Lord Judge.'

Faithful then asked for a chance to reply and Lord Hate-Good reluctantly agreed.

To his first accuser, the pilgrim said, 'All laws and customs that are contrary to God's word, are contrary to the Christian faith.' To his second he said, 'No worship can please God unless the faith of the worshippers is rooted in God's revealed will,' and to his third, 'The prince of whom you speak, and all his henchmen, are more fit for hell than for this town.'

Then the judge addressed the jury at length, concluding, 'With history on my side, I condemn this man to death.' This sentence was unanimously and speedily endorsed by the jury.

Faithful was taken from the courtroom to be beaten and punched, stoned and mocked, cut with knives and pricked with sword-points.

Finally, they tied him to a wooden stake and burnt him, as they thought, to death. They did not see, behind their backs, the chariot

and horses which swept courageous Faithful up through the clouds to heaven itself, as trumpets sounded.

Christian was returned to prison, but after a time, with God's help, he escaped. Then he continued with his journey, rejoicing in the knowledge that his former companion had passed beyond all torment and was tasting the joys of heaven, for which he also longed. Weak in body but strong in hope, Christian travelled onwards, singing about the pilgrim who had been faithful – even to death.

7.
DOUBTING CASTLE

opeful, an inhabitant of Vanity Fair, had decided to accompany Christian on his pilgrimage, and so the two men escaped from the town and hurried away together. Before long they overtook a man who, though secretive about his name, told them that he came from the Town of Fair-Speech, and would like to travel with them to the Celestial City.

'Is this Town of Fair-Speech a prosperous place? asked Christian.

'Indeed it is, and I have many titled relatives there,' the stranger replied. 'We are good, religious folk, though not as strict as some. We favour moderation and flexibility.'

These words gave Christian a clue as to the identity of their new companion, so he asked him, 'Are you called By-Ends?'

'That is the nickname given to me by my enemies, simply because I am flexible and progressive,' was the reluctant reply.

'If you want to travel with us, you must be prepared to go against wind and tide and be true to your faith, whether it brings you riches or poverty, popularity or persecution,' Christian told the speaker firmly.

By-Ends was not prepared to agree to this. 'You must not impose

your ideas on me,' he protested. 'Allow me my freedom and let me go with you.' But Christian refused to retract his conditions, and so By-Ends parted from them with the words, 'I will never betray my harmless and profitable principles. So, since I can't go with you, I'll keep to myself, until I find someone who will be glad of my company.'

When Christian and Hopeful had walked on until they were well ahead of By-Ends, they turned round, just in time to see him bowing ostentatiously to three gentlemen who had caught up with him. Their names were Hold-the-World, Money-Love and Save-All – former class-mates of By-Ends and ex-pupils of a man called Gripe-Man, from the northern country of Coveting. This schoolmaster had instructed his pupils in the art of getting what they wanted by fair means or foul.

These three men fell in beside By-Ends and asked him why Christian and Hopeful were walking on ahead.

'They want to keep travelling through all weathers and are prepared to lose all they possess on account of their pilgrimage,' By-Ends explained, 'but I thought that was rather extreme. I like to feel comfortable in my religion.'

Hold-the-World wholeheartedly agreed with this latter opinion. 'If God gives us good things, he surely wants us to keep them,' he reasoned.

Then By-Ends posed a question to his companions to help pass the time as they walked along together. 'If someone had the chance of obtaining the good things of this life and thus bettering himself, would he be justified in doing whatever was necessary in achieving that aim – including pretending to be more religious and zealous than he really was?' he asked. Money-Love replied at once that a person would certainly be justified in assuming an attitude of religious fervour in the cause of financial gain, and the others agreed enthusiastically with this answer. In fact, so certain were these four men that Christian and Hopeful would be of the same opinion, that they caught them up and, with Hold-the-World as spokesman, repeated By-Ends' question.

To this, Christian replied, incisively, 'To follow Christ for gain is wrong. Never, in any circumstances, least of all for the sake of self-preferment, could it be right to simulate faith and zeal. Besides, a man who takes up religion for the sake of worldly advantage, will doubt-less throw it down just as lightly.' Hopeful agreed with everything his friend had just said, but the four other men were dumbfounded. Seeing this, Christian and Hopeful turned and walked on. In a few moments, By-Ends and his companions followed – but at a distance.

'If they can't take criticism from another man,' Christian observed to Hopeful, 'how will they cope when they stand before God?'

The next stage of their journey took the pilgrims across the narrow Plain of Ease at the end of which was a little hill. Beside this stood a man, who began to call out as soon as Christian and Hopeful came into view, 'Come and see! There's a silver mine over here! Let me show it to you. With a little effort, you could soon be digging up riches for yourselves.'

The pilgrims stopped to look at the speaker. Hopeful was curious, and suggested that they should inspect the mine, but his companion replied, warily, 'I have heard of this place and of how many people have met their deaths here. Besides, riches are a snare to those who strive for them.'

Then Christian addressed the stranger. 'Isn't the ground near the mine dangerous?'

'Not very,' was the reply, but the pilgrims noticed that the speaker blushed as he said this.

'Let's be on our way,' Christian suggested to Hopeful. Overhearing these words, the man again begged the travellers to delay their journey just long enough to come over and look at the mine, but Christian

rounded on him for trying to entice them off the right way, and then said, 'Your name is Demas, isn't it?' When the man admitted that it was, Christian exclaimed, 'Now I know who you are! Your grandfather was Gehazi and your father the traitor, Judas, and you deserve to be hanged, just as he was!'

Without waiting for Demas' reply, the pilgrims continued on their way. Just before leaving the Plain of Ease, they looked back and saw that By-Ends and his companions were walking towards Demas' mine, which they then entered – to meet what fate the pilgrims could only surmise. Christian and Hopeful resumed their journey, but, coming across a pillar shaped like a woman, they stopped to read the words over the statue's head: 'Remember Lot's wife.'

This inscription made clear to the pilgrims that the monument had been erected to warn pilgrims against looking back covetously, as Lot's wife had done, and so been turned into a pillar of salt. The sight made Hopeful feel ashamed of his greedy impulse at the Hill of Lucre, and grateful that he had been spared the fate of Lot's wife. In this thoughtful frame of mind he walked along beside Christian. The pilgrims did not have far to go before they arrived at a delightful

stretch of countryside, which had been planned and landscaped especially for the benefit of travellers on their way to the Celestial City. Their path now lay along one of the banks of the River of the Water of Life, which was bordered by trees heavy with luscious fruit and bright with healing leaves. Beyond these fertile banks lay lush green meadows, luxuriant with lilies.

For several days and nights Christian and Hopeful remained in this haven, enjoying its delights and finding healing, nourishment and refreshment. Then they resumed their journey.

When the path and the river diverged, the going became difficult, and soon the travellers were footsore and tired. An inviting sight to the left made them pause. This was attractive By-Path Meadow. Christian noticed that the path which skirted this meadow seemed to be going in the right direction and promised easier walking conditions, so he suggested that they should take it. Hopeful was dubious about the wisdom of this idea, but he allowed himself to be persuaded by Christian's assurance that all would be well, and clambered over the stile on to the meadow path after him.

Once there, the pilgrims walked along together. Any doubts Christian might have had about their change of route were resolved when he called out to a fellow-traveller not far ahead, 'Where does this road lead?' and received the answer, 'To the Celestial Gate.' The man in front was called Vain-Confidence and the pilgrims began to follow him. But when night fell, they could no longer see to do this. Christian and Hopeful groped their way forward through the dark, but Vain-Confidence continued to stride ahead confidently and carelessly. Suddenly he tripped and fell, plunging headlong into

a deep pit that lay hidden in his path. The two men behind him heard the sounds and, guessing what had happened, stood still, calling out to Vain-Confidence as they did so, but a terrible groaning was all the reply they received.

'Wherever are we?' Hopeful cried out, but Christian, now very unsure of himself, gave him no answer. Then rain began to fall in torrents, while thunder snarled and lightning zigzagged overhead.

'How I wish we had not left our way!' Hopeful sighed. Christian was wishing the same thing, but he knew that they had taken the wrong path because of him, so now he asked for, and was freely granted, Hopeful's forgiveness. After that, there was no chance for further conversation as the travellers were fully occupied trying to fight their way back to the King's highway, but darkness and flooding prevented them from doing so, and only with great difficulty did they avoid being swept away and drowned. Finding at last a shelter of sorts, they threw themselves down under it, and fell into an exhausted sleep.

Next morning, they were roused by a loud and angry voice which demanded, 'Who are you and what are you doing in my grounds?'

Opening their eyes, Christian and Hopeful were confronted by the towering shape of Giant Despair. They replied that they were pilgrims who had lost their way. At this reply, the giant bellowed, 'You're trespassers on my land. Come with me!' Then he pushed them over the ground towards the grim, stone fortress known as Doubting Castle. There, he forced them through the door and down some steps into a stinking dungeon, where he left them.

That night he told his wife, Diffidence, about his new captives and asked her what he should do with them.

'First thing tomorrow,' she suggested, 'make yourself a crab-tree cudgel and beat them without mercy.'

Accordingly, in the morning, the giant entered the dungeon and began to abuse the prisoners, after which he beat them until they were almost senseless. All that day and night, Christian and Hopeful writhed and groaned in agony.

At bedtime, the giant again asked his wife what he should do to his prisoners. This time Diffidence suggested, 'Tell them that their best plan would be to kill themselves.'

In the morning, the giant visited the dungeon, and, with brutal bluntness, told the prisoners that, since they'd never escape, they should end their lives that very day by stabbing, hanging or poisoning themselves. Instead of agreeing to this, Christian and Hopeful asked the giant to release them. Their temerity so enraged their captor that his face contorted with hate and he rushed at the terrified pair. But before reaching them, he became uncontrollably convulsed, as often happened at the onset of one of the fits to which he was subject. This seizure rendered him powerless and saved the prisoners' lives – for the moment. After the giant's departure, Christian became so morbidly depressed that he suggested that they might as well obey the giant and put an end to their misery. Hopeful, however, pointed out that killing themselves would be tantamount to committing murder – an act forbidden by their Prince. 'Besides,' he added cheerfully, 'we

may yet escape, for I have heard of others who have been the giant's prisoners but have managed to break free, by God's grace.'

That evening, on finding that his captives, though barely breathing, were still alive, the giant flew into one of his terrible rages, after which he left the cell, saying ominously, 'You'll soon be wishing you had never been born!'

For some time Christian was in a state of stupor. When he was able to speak again, he repeated his suggestion that they should escape their present sufferings through suicide, but Hopeful, true to his name, reminded him of all the dangers he had already survived, adding, 'I, though weaker and younger than you, am enduring the same hardships; so have patience, my brother.'

That night, when the giant told his wife about the prisoners' irritating refusal to kill themselves, Diffidence put forward another of her unpleasant ideas.

'Take them to the palace courtyard and show them the bones and skulls there!' she suggested. So, in the morning, the giant led the prisoners to the courtyard and forced them to look at the gruesome human remains scattered over it.

'These are the bones of former pilgrims killed by me,' he told them, menacingly, then took them back to their dungeon, pummelling them every step of the way. As on previous nights, when they had gone to bed, Giant Despair and Diffidence discussed their captives. He voiced his surprise and annoyance at their continuing survival, but she, with uncanny perception, replied, 'Either they are nursing a secret hope of being rescued, or they have managed to hide a tool with which they mean, at the right moment, to pick the castle locks and so escape.' Promising his wife that the pilgrims would be minutely searched in the morning, the giant fell asleep.

Down below in their cell, the prisoners could not sleep, but at midnight they began to pray, and continued in this attitude until dawn, when Christian suddenly exclaimed, 'What a fool I've been! All this time I have had the means of escape right here with me!' So saying, he put a hand inside his coat and pulled out a bright object. It was the key of promise!

'Let's try it now,' suggested Hopeful, eagerly. With beating hearts, the pilgrims approached the door of their dungeon and tried the bright key in the lock.

It turned easily! The two men pushed the door ajar and stepped out: out from the den in which they had spent four days and three sleepless nights without food, water or light. Then, creeping up the stairs and over to the outer door, they tried the key again. Once more it turned smoothly in the lock, and the prisoners were able to open the door and slip silently out. Now only one barrier lay between them and freedom – the huge outer gates. They reached these without mishap, but this time the lock did not yield immediately to the key of promise. When at last it did, the pilgrims, forgetting caution, pushed hastily at the iron gates which began to creak alarmingly. Up in his bedroom, Giant Despair heard the sounds and sprang from his bed. As he moved however, one of his fits seized him, and prevented him from going any further. By the time he had recovered, the escaping prisoners had raced across the meadow, climbed back over the stile and regained the safety of the King's highway.

Before resuming their journey to the Celestial City, Christian and Hopeful spent some time in building, close to the stile, a pillar which they hoped would be a warning to future travellers. On this monument, they inscribed the words, 'Over this stile is the way to Doubting Castle, kept by Giant Despair, who despises the King of the Celestial City and wants to destroy his pilgrims.'

Then the pilgrims, singing as they walked, headed for the beautiful mountains which Christian had glimpsed from the roof of the Palace Beautiful.

8.
THE DELECTABLE MOUNTAINS

hristian and Hopeful arrived at the Delectable Mountains and found them to be as delightful as their name suggested. For some time they wandered about on the lower slopes, visiting gardens and bathing in rivers, drinking from fountains and eating from vineyards. Then, renewed and refreshed, they climbed to the upper slopes where they met four shepherds, whose names were Watchful, Sincere, Knowledge, and Experience. Leaning on their stout walking sticks, Christian and Hopeful asked the herdsmen, 'To whom do these mountains and flocks belong?'

They answered, 'The mountains form part of Immanuel's land; the Prince owns them, as well as these sheep for whom he laid down his life.'

Then Christian enquired, 'Is this the way to the Celestial City?'

'It is,' they replied.

Christian's next question was: 'Is the way ahead safe or dangerous?'

'It's safe for some, "but sinners stumble and fall in it," ' the shepherds answered.

'Is there refreshment available for weary travellers?'

'The Lord of the Mountain tells us to welcome strangers, so all the good things here are for your use,' was the gracious reply. Then the shepherds questioned the travellers about themselves and their journey. After listening to their answers, the herdsmen smiled warmly at them and said, 'Welcome to the Delectable Mountains!'

Then they escorted them to some nearby tents where they could eat and rest.

When they had eaten and rested, the pilgrims were taken by the shepherds on a tour of instruction among the hills and valleys. First the party climbed to the summit of the Hill of Error, one side of which was a sheer precipice. At its foot lay the smashed limbs and twisted bodies of climbers who had fallen over the edge. The shepherds explained to the appalled pilgrims that they were looking at the mangled remains of adherents to the false teaching of

Hymenaeus and Philetus, who insisted that the resurrection of the body had already happened. 'The bodies lie unburied as a warning to pilgrims,' the herdsmen concluded.

Next they were taken to the top of Mount Caution, from which they could see a distant graveyard. By focussing their eyes on this spot, they discerned the figures of some blind men who kept stumbling about among the tombs.

' "He that wandereth out of the way shall remain in the congregation of the dead," ' the shepherds quoted, adding 'The people you are looking at went over the stile into By-Path Meadow and so were captured by Giant Despair, who put out their eyes and deposited them among the graves where they have remained ever since.'

At these words, tears sprang into Christian and Hopeful's eyes, and they looked at one another, tacitly agreeing to say nothing of their own encounter with the dreadful ogre.

The shepherds then took the pilgrims to a grassy slope in which a door was set. When this was opened, the pilgrims looked down a dark tunnel from which came the roaring and crackling of flames, anguished cries and a burning, sulphurous smell.

'This is a by-way to Hell,' the shepherds told the shuddering pilgrims. 'It's for hypocrites and people like Esau, who sold his birthright, or Judas, who sold his master; it's also for blasphemers, like Alexander, and deceivers, like Ananias and Sapphira.'

'These men all began their journey to the Celestial City, didn't they?' Hopeful asked.

'Yes, and covered quite a distance, too,' was the reply.

The topic interested Hopeful. 'How far was it possible for them to go, in their time?' he asked.

'Some went further than these mountains, others not so far,' the shepherds answered.

'How much we need the Strong One's strength!' the pilgrims exclaimed to each other.

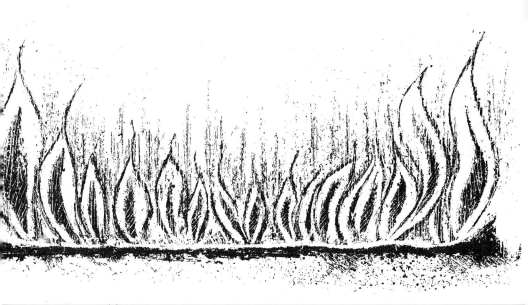

Christian and Hopeful were, by now, anxious to be on their way, so the shepherds escorted them to the end of the mountain range. Here they allowed the pilgrims to look through a telescope towards the distant Celestial City. Their view through the magnifying glass was not as clear as it might have been, for their hands were still trembling as a result of their glance down Hell's By-Way. In spite of this, they managed to catch a glimpse of the Celestial Gate and the glory surrounding it.

One shepherd then gave Christian and Hopeful a note with directions to the city, another said, 'Beware of the flatterer,' a third warned them not to sleep on the Enchanted Ground, and the fourth wished them, 'Godspeed.'

Having said goodbye to their helpful hosts, Christian and Hopeful descended the mountain-side, singing as they went.

9.
THE ENCHANTED GROUND

ear the base of the mountain, the pilgrims saw a youth stepping on to the King's highway. He had come from the Country of Deceit along a little crooked lane. This cocksure lad, named Ignorance, now fell in beside Christian and Hopeful as they headed for the Celestial City. After greetings had been exchanged, Christian asked the newcomer, 'How can you be sure that you will be received at the Celestial Gate?'

'I live a good life,' the young man replied. 'I pray, fast and give away money. I have even left home and country.'

'Yet, I'm afraid you will be treated like a thief and turned away at the Celestial Gate, because you didn't come on to the way through the wicket gate,' Christian said sadly.

Ignorance could not agree. 'You keep to your opinion and I'll keep to mine,' he suggested bluntly. 'No one in my country seems to know anything about this wicket gate. Besides, there is a perfectly good, green path leading from our country right on to the King's highway.'

Seeing that Ignorance had, for the present, closed his mind against them, Christian and Hopeful decided it would be wisest to leave him alone and give him time to reflect. So, for the next part of their journey, they kept well ahead of the youth.

Their way lay through a dark lane. Going along this, they were horrified to see a man, tied up with seven strong ropes, being carried by seven devils towards By-Way into Hell – the place recently visited by Christian and Hopeful.

As the group came nearer Christian thought he recognised the man as Turn-Away from Apostasy Town, and as they passed by Hopeful saw, from the inscription on the bound man's back, that he had once rashly made a profession of faith, but was now condemned as a renegade and a deserter. When the devils with their prisoner had

disappeared from view, Christian told Hopeful a story he had heard, about something that had happened in the dark lane along which they were travelling.

'Not long ago,' he began, 'a man called Little-Faith, from the Town of Sincere, came to this lane, but at its entrance, where Dead-Man's-Lane comes in from Broad-Way-Gate, he sat down and slept.

'Three men, brothers in blood and roguery, called Mistrust, Faint-Heart and Guilt, seeing the pilgrim waking from sleep and preparing to move on, shouted, "Stand still!" Little-Faith turned deathly white and obeyed, rigid with fear.

"Give me your purse," ordered Faint-Heart, and when the pilgrim did not immediately comply, Mistrust snatched a bag of silver from the man's pocket.

'At this, Little-Faith plucked up enough courage to shout, "Thieves! Thieves!" – only to receive a stunning blow from Guilt's cudgel. Someone could now be heard approaching the spot, and the thieves, afraid that this might turn out to be Great-Grace from Good-Confidence City, took to their heels, leaving Little-Faith on the ground, bleeding heavily. Recovering slightly after a time, the wounded man got to his feet and staggered on.'

'Did the thieves take away everything he owned?' asked Hopeful.

'Providentially they did not find his jewels or his scroll of admission to the Celestial City,' his companion answered.

'His jewels must have been a great comfort to him,' commented Hopeful.

'Not as great a comfort as they might have been,' replied Christian, 'for, from that time onwards, Little-Faith was obsessed by his misfortune, speaking and thinking of little else during the rest of his journey.'

An idea occurred to Hopeful. 'Why didn't Little-Faith pawn or sell his jewels?' he asked, brightly.

'Why, you bird-brain!' retorted his companion. 'To whom could he sell them, seeing they were not regarded as valuable in the country through which he was travelling? Besides, and even more to the point, he knew that if he did not present his gems at the Celestial City, he would not receive his inheritance there.'

This sharp response upset Hopeful who put forward an argument to justify his suggestion, but Christian soundly refuted this, and the younger pilgrim had to admit that his companion was in the right. Then Hopeful, still slightly nettled, demanded, 'Why didn't Little-Faith pluck up more courage and fight? These three rogues were probably cowards at heart.'

'Plenty of people talk like that, until they come face to face with them!' Christian remarked, 'and don't forget, these rogues are only trainee thieves, apprenticed to the King of the Bottomless Pit, and he stands ready to come to their aid at any time.'

He then told Hopeful that he knew all this from first-hand experience because he had encountered and resisted Mistrust, Guilt and Faint-Heart, but they had simply called on their master for help.

'I found it very hard to hold my own against *him,* though I was clad in armour from head to foot,' Christian concluded his tale.

'But they fled at the mere thought of Great-Grace!' persisted Hopeful.

'Ah, yes!' Christian agreed, 'but he is a King's champion and not every pilgrim is one of those! Little-Faith was only a weak pilgrim. And even Great-Grace has problems if those rogues manage to come to grips with him; his scarred face tells its own story. My advice is – don't ever wish to meet those thieves, or boast that you would have fared better than those who have had to face them. Our task is to wear all our armour, especially the shield of faith, "for with it, you will be able to put out all the fiery darts of the wicked." ' All the time they had been talking, Ignorance had continued to follow them, at a distance.

Now the pilgrims came to a path which joined theirs and seemed to be equally straight and true. As they hesitated, a dark man in a white robe came and greeted them. They told him of their predicament and he responded courteously, 'Follow me for I am going to the Celestial City, too.'

Flattered that a guide had apparently been sent to escort them, Christian and Hopeful followed the dark man down the path which joined theirs. For a short time all seemed well and then, suddenly, a net enveloped the two pilgrims, trapping them. As this happened, the white robe fell from their guide's shoulders and they saw who he really was. Too late they remembered the shepherd's warning, 'Beware of the Flatterer,' and the note with directions on it!

The Flatterer went away, leaving the two men he had led astray struggling to escape from their rope-prison. After a time, exhausted, they lay down and wept. Then they saw a Shining One, carrying a small whip, approaching them. First, he tore the net open and released the pilgrims. Then, having ascertained that they had been cautioned and given directions, he punished them for their carelessness and forgetfulness, saying, as he did so, ' "I rebuke and punish all whom I love. Be in earnest, then, and turn away from your sins." ' Far from resenting this treatment, Christian and Hopeful thanked the Shining One for his kindness. Then they retraced their steps to the right path and proceeded along it, singing of their recent, salutary experience.

Soon, a man coming from the opposite direction met the pilgrims, and asked them where they were going.

'To Mount Zion,' they replied. At this answer, the stranger, whose name was Atheist, burst out laughing.

'There's no such place as Mount Zion,' he sneered. 'I have been searching for twenty years and have not found it, so now I'm going back to enjoy all the pleasures I denied myself in order to pursue my quest.'

Christian, looking at Hopeful, asked, 'Does this man speak the truth?'

'Beware!' answered Hopeful, at once. 'He is one of the flatterers. In any case, didn't we see the gate of Mount Zion City from the Delectable Mountains? And aren't we supposed to be walking, by faith, towards it?'

Then Christian started to smile, delighted by Hopeful's reply, for he had posed the question simply to test his younger companion. At one in their rejection of Atheist, the pilgrims turned their backs on him and walked away. Before long the man's mocking laughter could be heard no more.

The air of the country through which the pilgrims had to travel next was noted for its soporific effect. Hopeful could hardly keep his eyes open, and suggested that they should take a nap, but Christian reminded him of the shepherd's warning against sleeping on the Enchanted Ground.

In order to keep awake and moving, Hopeful related the story of his past life.

'For many years I delighted in the follies of Vanity Fair,' he began, 'but then I heard, first from others, and later from you and Faithful, that these things bring death and condemnation. For a time, I tried to suppress the solemn thoughts which these words conjured up, because sin and the company of my friends still attracted me, and the awareness that I was doing wrong brought such depths of misery that I couldn't bear it – not realising that this was God's way of speaking to me. However, talking to good people, reading the Bible, hearing about someone's sickness or death and many other circumstances kept reminding me of my own impending death and the judgement that would follow.

'Then I tried to reform by turning from my sins, and performing many religious exercises, but I found no relief, for having rejected my former sins, I found myself committing new ones. Even my good deeds were spoiled by sinful elements. So my despair returned. Then I met Faithful, who told me I would never be saved unless I could possess the righteousness of a man who had never sinned. This man, he told me, was Jesus. Faithful also gave me a book and taught me how to pray to God for mercy. I read and prayed for a very long time, without finding any release. Then, one day, when I was feeling sadder than ever before, I saw and talked with Jesus – not with my bodily eyes and lips, but with my heart and understanding. He told me to believe and trust in him with all my heart, and promised that he would receive me, however great my sins, and make me right with God. Then I began to cry, out of sheer happiness, for now I understood how God could condemn the sin and justify the sinner. From

that moment, I turned, in shame and with loathing, from my old life and was filled with a longing to live a holy life, serving and loving my new Prince.'

When Hopeful had finished his story, he and Christian turned round and noticed Ignorance still in their wake.

So they waited until he had caught up with them. Then, although Ignorance made it clear that he didn't really want their company, the pilgrims fell in beside him and tried to draw him into conversation by asking him about his standing before God. Ignorance replied that his goodness must make him acceptable to God, and when Christian challenged this, the lad persisted, 'Surely a good heart, good thoughts and a good life are enough to please God.'

'But,' countered Christian, '*thinking* you have these things is not the same as actually *having* them. Besides, good thoughts and behaviour are only so if they agree with what God says on the matter – and in his book we read that no one is good.'

'But I'm not bad!' protested Ignorance. 'And I believe that Christ died for sinners and that it is he who, by his merits, makes my religious exercises acceptable to God.'

'You have entirely missed the point!' exclaimed Christian. 'It isn't our imperfect obedience that's acceptable to God; it's Christ's perfect obedience. His goodness, accepted by faith, covers all our sins.'

'But that's tantamount to saying, "Trust Christ and do as you please!"' protested Ignorance.

'You are certainly living up to your name,' sighed Christian. 'Can't you understand that saving faith produces love of God's name and word, his will and people, so that those who trust him will want to please him?'

Hopeful then made the point that no one could know God unless he chose to reveal himself to that person, but Ignorance scoffed at the idea of revelation. After that Christian made one more effort to make the lad understand his true condition, and urged him to turn to Jesus, by whose goodness alone he could hope to escape from condemnation.

To this Ignorance replied, 'You're going too fast for me. I'll walk behind for a while.' With these words, he slowed down, letting Christian and Hopeful go on ahead together.

As they walked along, the pilgrims talked sadly about the fate of Ignorance and many like him, who thought their own goodness would save them. Such people, they agreed, did, from time to time, experience conviction of sin, but they stifled their feelings of guilt – not realising that good could come out of them. At this point in the discussion, Christian was reminded of someone he had met years before. 'Did you know a religious man, called Temporary?' he asked Hopeful.

'Yes, I did,' his companion replied. 'He was a neighbour to Turn-back and lived in Graceless Town, two miles from Honesty.'

'That's the man,' Christian agreed. 'He began to feel the burden of his sins.'

'I know!' Hopeful interposed, 'For he lived three miles from me and often came and wept at my house. I felt sorry for him.'

'Once, he told me that he would even be prepared to become a pilgrim,' Christian continued, 'but then he met a man called Save-Self and I heard and saw very little of him after that.'

Then he asked Hopeful, 'Why do you think it is that some people begin to feel miserable about their sinful state, but don't do anything about it?'

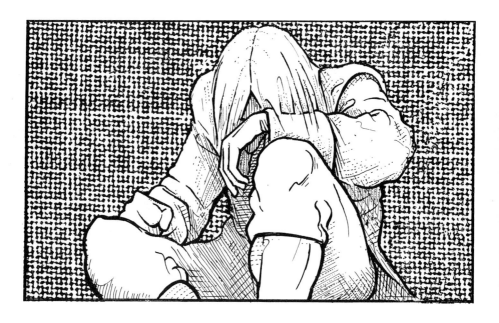

'I think their consciences are touched,' said Hopeful, 'but their minds and wills are unchanged. They fear their punishment, but don't detest their offences.'

'And so,' Christian continued, 'they stop thinking of God, death and judgement, as being subjects too painful to dwell on. Next, they stop all private and public practising of their religion, and start avoiding Christians, choosing, instead, the company of evil men, whose examples they soon copy.'

By this time, the pilgrims had completed their journey across the Enchanted Ground and arrived at the borders of a country more delightful than any they had ever seen.

10.
THE
CELESTIAL
CITY

his country was called Beulah: a land of heavenly joy, safe from the Valley of the Shadow of Death and Giant Despair, and within sight of the Celestial City. Here the air was vibrant with birdsong, and the earth glowed with flowers. Here the sun shone day and night, and the Shining Ones often walked and talked there, for it was on the borders of Heaven.

After entering this land, Christian and Hopeful wandered freely about, drinking in its beauty and feasting on its joys. Sometimes they heard voices from the Celestial City itself, exclaiming, ' "The Lord is coming to save you, bringing with him the people he has rescued," ' and at other times they were greeted by the inhabitants of Beulah with the words, 'You are among "God's holy people, the people he has saved." ' In this place of plenty, they feasted on corn and wine. High above the clouds, they glimpsed the Celestial City – but only through a special instrument; otherwise the sight of those golden streets, bathed in sunlight, would have blinded their mortal eyes. As it was, they saw, though dimly, the streets of gold and buildings of pearls and other gems, and were suddenly overwhelmed with love

and longing for that glorious place. These feelings were so intense that they brought about physical pain and sickness in the pilgrims, who were obliged to lie down and wait until the symptoms had eased.

When they felt better again, Christian and Hopeful continued to stroll through beautiful gardens, orchards and vineyards. At the gate of one of these vineyards, they met a gardener and asked him, 'To whom do these vineyards and gardens belong?'

'To the King,' the man replied. 'They are for his delight and for the refreshment of pilgrims.' Then he welcomed the travellers into the vineyard, letting them feast on its luscious fruit, before escorting them round the King's arbours and garden walks. Overcome at last by a pleasant feeling of drowsiness, the pilgrims lay down and slept, but even during their sleep, they were able to converse, freely and easily. This surprised them, until the gardener explained that the grapes always had this effect on people.

When they were fully awake, Christian and Hopeful got up, and begin to walk towards the golden city, taking care not to look directly at it. On the way they met two Shining Ones who asked them about themselves and their journey. Satisfied with the pilgrim's replies, the gleaming pair told them, 'There are now only two more obstacles between you and the city.'

The first was a deep river which flowed between the land of Beulah and the Celestial City. Christian and Hopeful could see no bridge across this. Seeing their surprise, the Shining Ones said, 'You must go through the water in order to reach the gate.'

'Isn't there any other way to the gate?' the pilgrims asked.

'Yes,' they replied, 'but only Enoch and Elijah were permitted to use it.'

Hopeful was beginning to feel dejected, and Christian even more so.

When they asked about the depth of the water, their guides answered, 'You will find it deeper or shallower according to your faith in the King of the place.'

At last Christian and Hopeful stepped hesitantly into the water. Immediately, the older pilgrim felt himself sinking, and shouted to his companion, who replied, 'Be brave, for I can feel the bottom, and it's firm.'

But dark horror enveloped Christian, and he could neither see clearly what lay ahead, nor recall any good moments from the past. Fear and guilt overwhelmed him. He was terrified by the thought of death and of being rejected at the Celestial Gate.

All the sins he had ever committed seemed to rise up and condemn him. Hallucinations in the shape of hobgoblins and evil spirits, added to his confusion and despair. All this time, Hopeful had been trying to comfort him as well as to keep his head above water. Now he said, 'Brother, I see the gate and men standing there to welcome us.'

'It's you, it's you they are waiting for!' cried Christian, in despair. 'Surely, if they had been waiting for me, my Prince would now be coming to help me. Instead, because of my sins, he's brought me into this snare where he will abandon me.'

But Hopeful answered, 'The wicked do not have such fears as yours. Your anguish does not mean that God has forsaken you; he merely wants to test you to find out whether you will remember how good he has been to you so far and will lean on him in your present troubles.' Christian still looked dazed, but Hopeful called firmly, 'Jesus Christ is making you whole and strong again!'

At these words, Christian's vision cleared and his depression lifted. Then he called out loudly and happily, 'I see him, oh, I see him, and he is saying, "When you pass through deep waters, I will be with you."'

So saying, he began to move forward with Hopeful through the water. The pilgrims soon reached the shallower part of the river and from there were able to wade ashore easily. As they gained the bank, they became aware of the fact that they had shed their mortal clothes.

The same two Shining Ones whom they had met before greeted them, then helped them up the steep hill, through the clouds, towards

the Celestial City. As they ascended, the heavenly guides described their destination.

'It is the paradise of God; within it stands Mount Zion, the heavenly Jerusalem,' they said. 'Its glory is indescribable. In it are countless angels. Abraham, Isaac and the prophets are there with all the spirits of good men made perfect. There you will meet with former friends. There you will eat the everlasting fruit from the tree of life. There, too, you will receive white robes and walk and talk with the King, the Holy One, whom, to your delight, you will see as he really is. Sorrow and sickness, trouble and death have no place in that city. Instead, you will know comfort and joy and reap the fruit of your tears, prayers and sufferings.'

As they travelled effortlessly higher and higher, the Shining Ones continued, 'You will wear golden crowns and praise the King perfectly and ceaselessly. Clothed with glory and majesty, you will ride a chariot splendid enough to be included in the King's triumphal procession, when he descends, on the wings of the wind, to judge the world. He will sit on his throne and you will sit beside him and help him pass sentence on all evil-doers. Afterwards, you will return with the King to the City, as trumpets sound, and stay with him there, for ever.'

By this time the gate was in sight and from it a company of Shining Ones came out to greet the approaching group. On hearing that Christian and Hopeful were pilgrims who had left everything for the love of their Lord, the welcome party sang out, 'Happy are those who have been invited to the wedding feast of the Lamb.'

This group was followed by the King's trumpeters, who made the heavens ring as they blew ten thousand welcomes to the pilgrims on their trumpets. So, surrounded by the glittering throng, Christian and Hopeful passed eagerly through the upper air, closer and closer to the Celestial Gate.

Soon they were close enough to read the words above it: 'Happy are those who wash their robes clean and so have the right to eat the fruit from the tree of life, and to go through the gates into the city.'

Looking down from the top of these gates were Enoch, Moses and Elijah, to whom the Shining Ones said, 'These pilgrims have come all the way from the City of Destruction, because they love the King of this place.' Then Christian and Hopeful presented their scrolls, which were taken and shown to the King. He commanded that the gates should be opened.

As the pilgrims, with radiant faces, stepped past the open gates and into the city, they were presented with golden robes and crowns to wear, and harps to pluck. Before them stood a host of Shining Ones, people and winged creatures, who had all assembled to greet the victorious travellers. Some played on their harps, others waved palm branches or sang melodiously.

'Come in and share your Lord's joy,' cried a voice, and all the city's bells added a harmonious peal of welcome. No longer able to contain their joy, Christian and Hopeful exclaimed, 'To him who sits on the throne and to the Lamb, be praise and honour, glory and might, for ever and ever!' Then the gates were shut.

Meanwhile Ignorance having reached the river, persuaded a ferryman to row him across. Arriving at the gate, he knocked and knocked. Finally, the men looking over the top asked him, 'Where have you come from? What do you want?'

'I have eaten and drunk in the King's presence and he has taught in our streets,' replied Ignorance.

The men then asked for his scroll and the traveller began to fumble in his clothes.

'Don't you have one?' the watching men asked, but received no

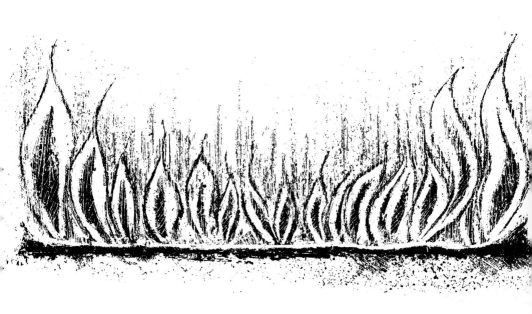

reply, so they went to the King and told him what had happened. He would not grant Ignorance an audience. Instead, he ordered two Shining Ones to bind him with ropes and carry him to a doorway which, even from the gates of heaven, led straight into hell.

And that's how the dream ended.